AF439293

Forced? Feminization

- An LGBT, Hot Wife, Forced Fem, Short-Read Romance

by Barbara Deloto and Thomas Newgen

Copyright Barbara Deloto and Thomas Newgen December 2021
The publisher and authors do not have any control over and do not assume
responsibility for third-party websites or their content. The reader has the sole
responsibility to use, or not use, the information contained herein, as well as for
the results of using this information. This is a work of fiction; any resemblances
to names or places are coincidental.
Cover photo by Vitalii Smulskyi on license from Shutterstock.com

To purchase another copy of this book, or to see our other books go to
https://www.amazon.com/Barbara-Deloto/e/B00J21HWA4/

A few of our other books
Realizing Jessica - A Femboy Gets Fem and Discovers Inner Passions and Love
Desires- Fantasy Becomes Reality for an Occasional Crossdresser
Trannies - Two Guys Get Fem
Jessica's Turn: A Gender-Bending LGBT Romance
Frat House - A Gender-Bending LGBT Romance
Finishing School - A Boy Is Sent to a Girls' Finishing School - An LGBT Romance
All Dolled Up: A Student Gets Fem - An LGBT Romance
Sissy Boyfriend
Being Candy
Paying My Dues
Virtual Vacation
Filling in For Her
His New Dress
Her Gift to Him
Telling Her
Feminized to Win
Crossdreaming
Feminized by Her
Taking it for the Team
Feminized Men: A Guide for Increased Joy in Crossdressing
Feminized Vacation
The House of Enchanted Feminization
Heirs to Heiresses
Connected
Our Gift to Each Other
Girlfriend
Insatiable
A New Taste for Life
Spellbound
Femboy Guild

1

"Aren't you ready yet, Billy?" my wife, Alex, asked as she clicked in her high heels and minidress to where I stood at the kitchen sink, trying to get the stain out of my pants.

"I must have gotten something on these the last time I wore them. I need to buy more dress pants for nights like this."

She looked at the stain and took the sponge from my hand. "Forget it, honey. That's not coming out. You can wear a pair of my pants."

"Your pants? They'll know."

"No, they won't. It'll be our little secret. C'mon." She tugged me by the hand into the bedroom. "First, let's have some fun tonight." She took out a pair of sheer black pantyhose.

"No way! I'm not wearing pantyhose."

"Shush!" She cut out a piece of the crotch. "Put these on."

I can never say no to her. She's so smart. Being a psychiatrist, she always gets me to do anything she wants anyway. I took them and slid onto the bed, removed my tighty-whities, and slid my hairless legs into them. I always shaved my body hair—I felt so much cleaner without it.

"That's it, Billy. Now slip these on." She handed me stretchy, high-waisted black lace panties. I slid them up, and my arousal showed as I tucked it into the panties. I could tell my face was flushed. I tilted my head down and looked up at her.

She held my chin and kissed my forehead. "Now don't be embarrassed. It feels nice, doesn't it? Much nicer than your boring guy clothes... Right, Billy?"

I nodded. She handed me the pants, and I slid into them. They were black and had a side zipper. I slid them over my hips, and the zipper snugged them nicely. I slid on her belt.

"Alex, look at how clearly the smooth front shows me under it."

"No one will see that with your coat on. And see? A perfect fit. You're the same size as me, just a teeny bit less hippy. Take your shirt off." She went to the drawer and pulled out a black lace bra that matched the panties.

"Honey, no! They'll see it under my shirt."

"Nonsense. Besides, the way your breasts have been growing the last couple of years, you should wear a bra anyway. You'll have nice cleavage, and it'll feel nicer than strapping them down all the time." She wrapped the bra around my chest and clasped it, then made me slip my arms through the straps. She adjusted my breasts in the cups, sending a tingle though me. "There. Now put your shirt back on and your sport coat, and you'll be all set. No one will know."

She went back into the closet and came out with some of her black penny loafers with a thick, three-inch heel. "Here. These will give you a couple more inches." She knelt down and held them as I slipped my feet into them. She stood and adjusted my coat and hair. Oh good, you wore your diamond stud earrings. Perfect. You look so cute all dressed up like a little man."

"Little man. Thanks a lot. And even worse, *like* a little man —as if I weren't a man."

She bent down and kissed my forehead, taller than me in her very high heels. "But you *are* a cute little man. The little man I love. So what if you've never been very manly? I still say you'd make a lovely girl. Now let's go to the party. You need to accept your award."

I checked myself in the mirror and I looked normal, but with the clothes I was wearing, I couldn't help but feel more like a girl than a guy. The pressure and crush of the bra and the silky feel of the pantyhose and panties kept me aroused. Luckily, as Alex had said, it didn't show under the sport coat. I checked my ponytail in the back to be sure it was together well. "Okay. Ready."

"Okay, honey. Now let's go party!"

Alex drove in her heels and minidress, and I couldn't help glancing at her silky, stockinged legs as they moved on the pedals. She wore a smile and slid her hand onto my thigh. "See? Doesn't this feel nice? Maybe we can have a little party of our own later." She slid her hand onto my crotch and rubbed my hardness. "Mmm, your little thingy is happy. That's so adorable."

I gazed out the window, trying to make it go down, but her hand rubbing it was only making it worse. I crossed and recrossed my legs, but she was persistent, and my silky legs slipping against each other made it even worse. I gasped and took her hand away. "Hey, stop, or I'll have another stain... on your pants this time."

She placed her hand with its long, pink-painted nails on the steering wheel and laughed. "Oh, yeah. Now I remember how that stain on your pants got there last time. I had a smoke outside with Dan at our house party, and then I sat on you and gave you a little lap dance. I was so horny that night, and something oozed from my panties."

I nodded. "Oh, yeah. Dan. I remember seeing you against the wall on the patio with your dress hiked up, and there he was, our next-door neighbor, ramming it into you while you smoked. Wow, that was a crazy night, wasn't it? I didn't know how to act with you getting pounded by all the guys. I mean, it was exciting to see but... you know."

"I know. You felt insignificant and insufficient, but the excitement made up for it. I still say you'd feel better presenting as a woman, and then you wouldn't be having all these little-man syndrome issues."

"I don't have little-man syndrome issues. I never try to make up for it by being macho like little men do."

"Not like that, but you know you're more suited to be a woman. Now that you've grown breasts and added more soft curviness to your hips and legs, you should be even more sure of the fact. Why your brain is fighting with old paradigms is beyond me. We could both be indulging in those *real* men, not just me. You'd find greater purpose and pleasure being able to please someone like that. I know you would. You'd love to give pleasure to others."

I stared out the window and recrossed my silky legs as I throbbed uncontrollably while thinking of being like my wife.

"I know it's exciting for you to think about. Admit it."

I shook my head. "No. I won't think of it. I'm a man."

"Okay, Billy. If you say so. It worked out well, though, didn't it? We all had a great time. I remember how fast you finished when I gave you that lap dance, and you felt my wetness through your pants, knowing it all came from real men. Good thing I can't have babies, huh?"

She pulled into the country club. The valet took the car, and we went inside. We had dinner and drinks and played proper conservative people. I gave my little speech, accepted the award for most patented software releases the past year, and we had dessert and left.

The valet brought the car around and we got in. "Okay, honey. The night is young. Let's go celebrate your award at a really fun place." Alex checked her watch. "Everyone should be at the dance club by now, waiting for the guest of honor."

"Who'd you invite?"

"Just a few of the guys from our last house party."

"Dan?"

"Him and a couple of the other guys who were there that night. I hope you don't mind, Billy. I just thought you might like to see our fun friends tonight."

"Of course, honey. Of course."

She threw a flat-lipped smile at me, then wriggled her bottom in her car seat. "This will be so much fun. You're a sweetie, Billy."

2

We walked into the dance club; the music pounded out a sexual beat. Dan, Mike, and Pete came right over. Dan slapped me on the back and thrust his hand into mine, crushing it. "Congratulations, little buddy. You won. Nice job!" Mike and Pete followed suit, and drinks appeared in our hands. Dan put his arm around Alex and pulled her close to him. He held his drink up to us all. "To keeping the juices flowing for Billy!"

Juices flowing? I'm sure he meant my creative juices, or did he mean his, Mike's, and Pete's juices into Alex?

Alex lifted her glass. "To lots of juice!" She tossed the martini down. I sipped mine.

We found a booth, and Dan and Mike flanked Alex. Pete sat next to Mike, and then I was on the outside next to Pete. When Alex wasn't drinking, she had both hands under the table, and it was obvious to me what she was doing with them. Mike and Dan seemed to take turns with their hand under Alex's dress, making her squirm and giggle.

Pete and I basically watched and sipped our drinks. "So, Billy, your wife is really cool, and you seem to be too. So are you guys swingers?"

"Uh, not really." I recrossed my legs, tucking my hardness between my thighs. "Just sometimes."

He nodded. "Well, I think it's really great that a guy like you can let his wife have real men. I mean... you know... I mean letting regular guys meet her needs. I don't mean you don't satisfy her but... I mean... Uh, sorry."

"No. That's okay. I guess it's okay to talk about it. I mean, I'm not the most masculine guy around, you know?"

He nodded quickly, his eyes wide. "Right. I mean, we are what we are, right? You're a good-looking guy too. Just not built like a guy so much. I mean, you have great facial features and a nice thin body. If you were a girl, you'd be gorgeous. I mean... you know."

"Yeah. So I've been told. Not that I haven't thought the same thing. I mean..." I looked around the club. Everyone was busy with Alex, and no one around us was looking our way. I put my hand on Pete's leg and leaned into him and whispered. "Look into my shirt." I looked around and then undid one button and showed him my cleavage.

His eyes popped open. "Wow. Those are nice. You sure you're a guy?"

"Well, I do have the appendage."

"Does it work?"

"It works very well, thank you."

"Wow. That's a dream come true. The best of both worlds. You must make yourself horny with those boobs."

I nodded and sipped my drink. "Showering always leads to entertainment and well, you know... relief. Once that happens, though, I'm okay the rest of the day... mostly."

His eyes wide, Pete nodded as he took my face in, his eyes flitting back and forth between my chest and face. "You should present as a girl all the way. Really."

"Ya think? I'm a guy, though, and I like girls, not guys."

"You sure? How did you get those boobs anyway? They don't just grow on trees."

I rolled my eyes. "I know. They just started growing. After we got married. I think they're as big as they're gonna get, though. They've been this way a few months now."

He nodded. "And your wife's a psychiatrist, right? They can write prescriptions, right? She ever write one for you for hormones?"

"No. But she does have me take vitamins every day. At least she says they're vitamins. Hmm…"

Pete nodded.

I sipped my martini and whispered to him, "Could she be slipping me hormones? Why not? I'd never know. Gosh. She's been trying to turn me into her girlfriend since we got married."

"If she did, I think she did a good thing, from the results I'm seeing."

Pete and I watched Alex. She, Dan, and Mike dashed off, with her tugging Dan by his hand as she clicked off in her heels. Pete nodded. "You okay, Billy? You got quiet."

"Just thinking... I wonder if Alex might have given me hormones."

"Well, do you like your breasts?"

I looked around then slid a hand under my coat and felt one. Squeezing it felt delicious. I nodded. "I guess I really do. I mean, at first I was really scared, but Alex said it was okay and there was nothing wrong with me, and I should get used to them and I did. I hate always strapping them down so they don't show. Not very comfortable. I do love when she pays attention to them in bed."

"Do you wish they were gone?"

"Heck no."

"Then whether she slipped you hormones or not is a moot point. If she did, she did it to please you, and if she didn't, she helped you accept and enjoy them. It's all good, right?"

I placed my hand on his thigh and squeezed it. "I guess you're right."

He placed his hand on mine, gazing lovingly into my eyes. "Good. You're *soo* pretty, Billy." He slid my hand to his crotch and pressed it against his huge hardness. I felt him throb beneath my hand, and I throbbed in my panties. My heart raced. His breath in my ear was hot as he whispered, "Be the girl you are, Billy. Be the girl you are."

3

I couldn't stop myself from feeling the hardness I elicited from Pete. It was strangely exciting to think I made him feel that way, yet my brain told me to let go and be a man. I gave it one last squeeze, feeling the firm heft of it. I rubbed it. I gave it one more last squeeze. Then I rubbed it again. I squeezed it again.

Thank goodness, Pete pulled my hand aside. But then he made things worse and unzipped his pants, took it out and wrapped my fingers around it. It was *soo* silky and smooth, hairless and hard. My heart raced and I couldn't stop myself from stroking it. It felt so wonderful to grip it and know I was sexy to him and making him feel like that.

"That's it, Billy. See how nice it feels? Your hand is so tiny and soft; it feels so warm on it. You're making me feel tremendous. Does it feel nice to you?"

I gazed around the club, nodding quickly. My brain was telling me to stop, but I couldn't. It didn't feel nice. It felt *incredible*.

I couldn't stop stroking it and squeezing it. It felt so sensual. "Pete, I shouldn't be doing this. It's wrong." I kept stroking it uncontrollably, almost wishing he'd stop me so I wouldn't have to fight myself over it.

"There's nothing wrong with a girl taking care of a man's needs."

I stopped stroking and held it. "A girl?"

"Yes, Billy. You're a girl. Please, don't stop, honey."

I sped up my stroking.

"That's a good girl, Billy. Take care of your man."

I used my other hand and tugged on his shaved, silky globes.

"Atta girl, use both hands. Be ready, though. You've gotten me very excited, and I might not be able to hold back much longer."

He looked around, then slid his hand under my sport coat and squeezed my breast. It sent tingles through me.

"Oh, Pete. I should stop. You need to save it for Alex. She'll want you next."

"Don't worry. I'll be ready again soon, and I'll be able to last longer for her. I want you to feel what an exciting, sexy girl I think you are." He slid his hand under my shirt and bra and pinched my nipple. He kissed my neck and let out a little moan. His body went rigid in his seat. He looked into my eyes and nodded, then squeezed my breast hard and kissed my forehead.

I felt his shaft swell in my hand.

4

Pete's legs tensed as I gently tugged on his globes and squeezed his shaft. He humped lightly into my grip, and I felt the shaft jerk and swell as it shot a gush onto my shirt. I couldn't help shuddering as I came in my tight panties. Another gush from him and another from me. I whimpered meekly. He kissed my forehead and let a little groan out. "Oh my god, Billy, you're such a gorgeous girl. You make me feel so good."

He breathed deeply as the last pulses of his juices shot through my grip and onto my shirt. It was so thrilling, feeling him do that over me. Feeling it flood through my hand and onto my shirt. My body tensed, my heart raced, and I kept gushing into my wife's panties beneath her pants. I whimpered as the last shots soaked my panties, and Pete gently kissed my forehead.

He tucked himself away and handed me a napkin. I smeared his juices over my shirt and buttoned my sport coat as I slid out of the booth and went to the men's room.

I stared at my eyes in the mirror for a moment, wondering who I was inside, then washed my hands and went into a stall. I dried my panties as best I could with toilet paper. I was shocked at what had happened. My heart was finally starting to settle down. I sat down and tried to pee, but I was still too hard to manage anything. I wasn't getting soft, and the more I thought about it, the readier I was for more. I was an animal—sensual, alive, and driven. The way Pete excited me, I had to be a girl inside. I loved every second of it, and I wanted more.

I left and walked out back for a breath of fresh air. Off in the distance, there was a dark corner with high-top tables and a couch. I could see Alex lying on the couch, Mike thrusting into her face while Dan held her legs, her high-heeled feet flailing as he pounded himself into her over and over. She moaned around Mike's shaft as he held her head and thrusted into her face.

Alex shuddered and her leg twitched. She let out a muffled moan. Mike held her head tight and lifted his head to the sky as his knees wobbled and he shot his load into her face. Dan grunted and held her hip with one hand as he shoved his thick, long, glistening rod deep into her. He held it there while he crushed one of her breasts with the other hand. Her body shuddered while Mike released all his passion into her. I was throbbing in my panties watching how good Alex felt being taken by those two handsome and masculine men.

Mike took himself out of her mouth and tucked away. Her head rolled to the side. She saw me and smiled as Dan withdrew himself from her tight, oozing depths and returned it into his pants. She stood, adjusted her panties and licked her fingers, then straightened her mini dress. She clicked over to me, her hips swaying, a big grin on her face. She wrapped her arms around my neck and gave me a deep kiss, forcing into my mouth a good amount of what Mike had deposited into her face. We kissed deeply, the taste of it and thought of the immense pleasure he had had with my wife made me even more aroused. I even felt a pang of jealousy. Not over other men having made her feel so good, but because I wasn't her.

She leaned back and took stock of me. I had forgotten to button my sport coat, and in the dim light of the moon, she reached down and felt the damp spots smeared on my shirt. She felt my hardness through her pants and grinned. "Did you mess on yourself, little girl?"

"Uh, I... um, not me... I mean... Well, I did mess your panties but the shirt...Well, it was..."

"Pete? Did you make Pete finish? And you finished while you were doing that?"

"Uh, I didn't mean to, mess your panties that is, or have Pete mess my shirt. I told him not to so he could save it for you. But he said he'd be ready for you quickly, and then he'd last longer for you."

"I guess that'll do. Hmm, so tell me. Did you use your hand or your mouth?"

"Just my hand. I'm sorry. I couldn't stop myself. Pete was so nice, and I just got carried away. I told myself to stop and all but..."

She put her long-nailed finger on my lips. "Hush, little girl. I'm happy for you. I'm especially happy and proud of you that it was so exciting for you, doing that to Pete, that you couldn't help letting it all go in my panties. Now you *must* know you're an attractive enough girl to excite a man like Pete, and you're not even dressed like one. Except underneath. Now are you ready to be a real girl and stop masquerading as a man?"

"Uh, no. Not really."

"Oh, honey! Well, I guess we should all go back and have another drink, and then I can bring Pete out here and take care of him, and you can watch and think about how good that would be for you to have it done to you. Dan made me sore in front, so now it's time for Pete to use the backdoor to make *his* deposit."

"Back door?"

"Sure, honey. The same way a man would make love to you. It's as good if not better than the front. Trust me. You're gonna love it."

"I, uh... Please Alex. I don't think so."

"You'll at least watch us, won't you? Dan and Mike are leaving now that they got their rocks off with me. You may as well watch and see what it'll be like for you, or you'll be all alone inside. Unless you want to be by yourself and pick up some other man to please. That would be fine too." She winked.

"If those are my choices, I think I'd rather just watch."

"Good girl." She kissed my forehead. "Now imagine I'm you with Pete."

And I did. Pete took her in her bottom from behind and from in front with her heels behind her ears. It was as exciting as seeing her with Dan and Mike, and I couldn't help thinking about me being her and having Pete do that to me. It was frighteningly exciting, but even so, I wasn't ready for it. My self-image wasn't ready to become that much of a girl.

Alex drove, the cool breeze blowing in our hair. "So, girlfriend, ready for being a girl like that, ready to please a man that way?"

"Oh Alex, please. I'm so overwhelmed right now."

"Aren't you still aroused? I know you finished again in my panties watching Pete and me, because I saw you rubbing your pants and shaking when I came on him and he came in me. But I know your libido doesn't stop or drop off from finishing like it does for men."

"How would you know that?"

"The same way I gave you breasts, Billy. Your 'vitamins.'"

"Is that why every morning I have to get rid of it in the shower?"

"Of course. I wanted you to be happy with your breasts, and that was a way to make you enjoy them more."

I nodded. "I did figure out you were giving me hormones, by the way."

"Are you mad at me?"

"No. Pete and I discussed that, and it doesn't really matter because I love my breasts and the softer shape of my body."

"So you're ready to be a girl now?"

I shook my head.

"We'll see. Trust me. I know what's best for you."

5

The next day I made breakfast for us, and then Alex had me shave my whole body. I usually did that anyway, but then she had me use the attachment in the shower to clean out my bottom. (I'd always wondered what it was for…)

After my shower, she did my makeup and lipstick and styled my hair for a feminine look. In the bedroom, she had me stand in front of her while she held my shaft with her thumb and forefinger and took it daintily into her mouth. It was heaven. She stroked the bottom inch with her thumb and forefinger and ran her tongue around the other couple of inches and the tip while bobbing and sucking.

She stopped and looked up at me, her eyes gleaming. "Now imagine I'm you, just like you did last night. Imagine doing this but to a nice, thick, long, hard, silky one, on a man, say it's Pete." She went back at it, her eyes on mine as she sucked and ran her tongue around it and across the tip, making me spasm.

She tugged my hairless golf balls and bobbed her head. I imagined doing that to Pete, and I instantly started to release. Just then, Alex shoved something slick up my butt. I came violently, wriggling on the thing inside me and humping Alex's face like a rabbit. I whimpered and my knees went weak and shaky. She sucked my juices away and swallowed them while the thing she shoved into me began to hum and swell.

When I had stopped gushing, she stood. "There. All plugged and almost ready. I left out one pill from your vitamins this morning, so you should lose your hardness right now." She went to the dresser, took something out, and came back. She slid my globes and softening rod through a ring, then quickly pressed a pink plastic cap with a hole in it over my shaft and locked it to the ring.

She took her phone and tapped on it a few times with her fingers. The cage began to send little electric shocks through my rod, making it jerk on and off and begin to swell again. The next thing I felt was the plug vibrating and sending buzzing shocks into my bottom. There, how does that feel?"

"Uh, weird. Sensual. Arousing. Electric. Do I have to keep these on?"

"Yes. Until you finally decide to be a girl. The electric feeling is correct. The both have vibration and e-stim. It's not too strong, is it?" She played with her phone.

"Ouch."

"Better?"

"That's feels nice there." I felt the plug's e-stim and vibration get more intense. I grabbed her shoulder.

"Good?"

"A little much."

"Good. Better for it to be a little more than just nice." She put her phone away. "Oh, your pill."

She went to the nightstand and grabbed my water glass then took a pill from her purse. "Take this. You can have your libido pill now that the cage is on."

"But honey, I really don't need one."

"Take it. I want you maxed out so you're properly motivated today. Sit on the bed and I'll get your clothes. We're going to the mall."

I sat and she painted my toenails a metallic pink then dried them with a hairdryer. She brought me sheer suntan pantyhose, a matching pink bra and panties, a denim miniskirt and short-sleeved pink V-neck sweater with a pair of high-heeled, sand-colored wedge sandals. When I was dressed, she put on rings, bracelets, and a necklace and replaced my stud earrings with long dangly ones. She held me at arms' length and checked me out. She adjusted my breasts in the bra and sprayed perfume all over me. "There. How do you feel?"

"Uh, horny, sexy, feminine, and longing for a release. Please, can I? Please undo the cage and let me."

"That's good, but don't be silly. You can't finish until you commit to being the girl you are. Now let's go to the mall and get you some more piercings, clothes, and makeup and get your hair and nails done. You're not going to have a choice anymore but to be seen as a sexy girl. Enough fighting your silly old paradigms. You aren't a man and never will be."

She placed my things in a purse and slung it on my shoulder. "March, little girl."

I walked out, the plug shooting off and making me shake my hips, the cage shooting off and my rod filling and straining against it in my panties. My breasts tugged on my chest, jiggling my creamy cleavage with each step. I didn't know how I could get any more girlish by going to the mall.

I stopped. "Honey, we don't need to go to the mall. I'm feminine enough, aren't I?"

"Almost. I want you to have styled hair and long fake nails so there's no way you can wear your boy clothes and look anything like one. Everyone has to see you as a girl from now on because that's who you are." She kissed my lips lightly. "I love you, my wife, Billy."

6

If it weren't for the plug and cage, it would have been a wonderful day, actually... I think. The girls in the salon were so nice! They were so hot and sexy too. I would have loved to have taken the cage off and stuck it into either of them, or both, one after the other. I'd have finished in just a jab or two if I could get it in them. Their hands in my hair and handling my fingers and hands felt like an orgy of caresses, and they were the epitome of sexiness.

I was constantly on the edge with the double whammy of stimulation and being in the cage. I was starting to embrace the sexy young girl I was, feeling so pretty and feminine. The haircut with highlights and colors framed my face beautifully. My very long nails, painted to match my toenails peeking from the strappy wedge heels, made my fingers look so pretty doing anything they did. I couldn't wait to see them wrapped round Pete's gorgeous meat.

Alex paid as the girls gave me hugs and kisses and fussed with my hair, telling me how to take care of it. We left the salon.

"I think you really love the new you. Do you?"

"It is pretty. I love the feel and look of the nails and the haircut. Thanks." I walked, feeling the jiggle of my breasts and my hips slightly swaying in the high wedges. My head was held high as we made our way through the mall holding hands.

"Glad to hear that. So now you must be totally ready to be a girl. Right, Billy?"

I rolled my eyes. Alex stopped and looked in the window of a store where a sexy minidress was on display. "Oh, look. I want to see you get laid in that. C'mon, sweetie." She tugged me into the store.

We shopped until we dropped. Alex bought me all sorts of sexy clothing, heels, underthings, jewelry, hair accessories, makeup, perfumes. I was like a kid in a candy store, loving all the new and interesting looks I now had as options. Alex forced me to get two more lobe piercings and one cartilage piercing as well. She said no guy wears that many, so I needed to have them to further separate myself from any thought of being a male.

By the end of the day, I was ready to rest. My panties under the miniskirt were damp from the constant oozing from all the stimulation. I just wanted to finish and go to sleep.

"Okay, Billy. Let's get your new things put away, and then we can go out. I'll call the boys if you want, or we can find some new entertainment. You can choose."

"Gosh, Alex. I mean, I'm beat and I'd just like to take it easy. Can't you take me out of these torture devices and just let us go out as wife and wife? Please? I think I'd like to be the girl I am now with just you. I love you even though, and maybe because, you've done this to me. But I've always loved you. Please can we not rush this goal you have for me and just enjoy each other? I can't present myself as a guy anymore anyway. There's no rush." I ran my long, painted nails through my hair and smiled at her. "Pretty please? Just us girls? Haven't I been a good girl?"

She rolled her eyes, then smiled at me and ran the soft back of her hand against my cheek. Her eyes flitted around my face, hair, and new piercings. "Well, since you're calling yourself a girl and acting like one, and you did such a good job of allowing your presentation to become so unmistakably female, I suppose it wouldn't hurt to let you have a little reward and relax a little before we finish your induction into womanhood with the men's lust-filled deposits. You win."

I jumped up and down and clapped my hands. "Thank you, thank you, thank you, honey. You're so sweet."

I stood there in the bedroom and hiked up my skirt. "Unlock me please."

"Oh, Billy."

7

"Let's get your outfit together first." Alex led me into the closet and selected my clothes. "There."

"Honey, that dress doesn't leave much to the imagination."

"Exactly. It's the perfect LBD. And you'll have to be careful how you sit. It'll be good for you—it will force you to try to be modest in such a slutty dress. Besides, no guy will pass you by when you're wearing that."

"Exactly. I just want to relax."

"You'll be fine." She put a black lace garter belt, sheer black push-up bra and matching panties, sheer black stockings, fetishy-high, strappy black stilettos, a matching purse and bracelets, rings, necklace, ankle bracelets, and perfume on the bed. "That should look wonderful on you, and you'll smell like a dream."

I stared at it all. "Okay, I guess. But the cage and plug please?"

She flattened her lips as she looked at me. "Hmm."

"Please? Pretty please?"

"I don't know. You've been so compliant today and good while wearing those things that I'm not sure I want to let you free of them yet."

"Oh honey, *please*."

"I'll tell you what. We'll compromise. You can take the plug out, but the cage stays for now. Will that be a help, or do you want to keep the plug in too?"

"That's my only choice?"

"Totally your choice. Both or just the cage."

"How about take the cage off and leave the plug?"

"Uh, sorry. We both know what will happen as soon as the cage is off. Right? You'll not restrain yourself from finishing over and over. You'll be squirming and touching yourself all the time. It'll be embarrassing for you out in public like that, not to mention very messy."

"I promise not to. I'll be good. Just let me take it off and take the plug out and just finish once."

"Hmm. There should be something you can trade for me letting you do that. Something to help prove you're more of a girl inside now too."

"Anything. Please?" I stood there looking helpless as the cage and plug kept up their relentless patterns of vibration and e-stim. My skin tingled all over. A drip came from my cage now and again, further soaking my panties. "Please, Alex! I'll do anything."

"Okay. Then you'll have a man make love to you."

I rolled my head on my shoulder. "Oh, Alex, please not that. Not yet."

"See? Gosh, Billy. You're making this so hard."

She started to change into her outfit for dinner. It was a more conservative businesslike suit dress that made her look like the doctor of psychiatry she was. I sat on the bed, frustrated and deflated, my head hung low, staring at my pretty toenails in the strappy heels, my legs crossed and bouncing a leg over the other.

She finished dressing, sprayed perfume on, and sat on the bed next to me. "Don't look so sad. You know I'm trying to help you, honey."

"I know."

She ran her hand through my hair and lifted my chin, then kissed me lightly on the lips so as not to mess our lipstick. "Okay. If you won't let a real man breed you, then let's take a step at a time. You'll need to finish one off using your mouth tonight. Agree?"

I imagined doing Pete like that, and it made me ooze. "Okay. Okay. That I can do. Can we meet Pete?"

"We'll see. It might not be Pete, but we'll see. If not him, you still have to do it, or the consequences will be a much longer time before any relief comes again."

"Okay, I promise."

Alex lifted the hem of my minidress and pulled aside my panties. She unlocked the cage and took it off. It sprang to attention and jumped up and down uncontrollably in the cool air. From her nightstand she grabbed a realistic strap-on dildo I used on her when I wanted to make love to her. She handed me a pair of pink ruffled panties. "Use these and think of Pete in your mouth." She stuffed the dildo in my mouth and held my chin as she thrusted it in and out.

My little thing jumped and leapt in the cool air, and I thought of how good Pete would feel in my mouth as he came. I whimpered and spurted before the pretty sissy panties even touched it. I wrapped it in the silky fluff, and my body shook while I whimpered throughout shooting my long-awaited gushes into the panties.

I jerked it wildly in the silkiness. Alex smiled and patted me on the head. "Good girl." She removed the dildo. "Now that's it. Get all of your little sissy release out of you so you can make a real man fill your mouth with his passionate release. Right, princess?"

I nodded quickly, still terribly excited with the thought of doing that to Pete. I couldn't stop jerking myself with the fluffy panties as I imagined my goal for the evening. I whimpered some more and rolled my head on my shoulders. I whined, "Oh god... god, yes! I want it." The plug cycled on and off, triggering the emissions I deposited into the pink panties.

Finally, I finished jerking myself into the panties, and my body relaxed. I took a deep breath. "Oh god. Thank you, Alex. That was *soo* good. I needed that."

Alex put her arm around my shoulders and pulled me tight to her as she kissed my cheek. "You're welcome, honey. Now tuck that little thing in your tight panties and let's go."

"But the plug. I want to take the plug out. Please? Let me just be me, okay? I promise to do what we agreed on, okay? Please?" I whimpered.

"Hmm."

8

Alex let me take the plug out. Thank god! But she made me take another libido pill before we left. I thought it was a fair trade. At least I was somewhat free in my tight panties versus the darn electric cage, and I didn't have the constant stimulation of jolting shots in my bottom.

We went to dinner at a very upscale restaurant. Luckily, Alex had me wear a crop top that would make my hard nipples less obvious, and I managed to keep the hem of my dress covering the lace tops of the sheer black stockings. I still looked pretty darn slutty but classy enough for the restaurant. I felt immensely alluring and feminine, and the contrast to my normal male-mode mental state was more than pleasant and rewarding.

Alex held my hand at the dinner table, gazing into my eyes. Her other hand caressed my stockinged leg beneath the table. "You're coming along well, Billy. I'm proud of you. How do you feel about it now?"

I looked to the ceiling, weighing my emotions and feelings. "Uh, I happen to love how good I feel about my self-image right now. I feel more in my skin than I ever did before. I mean I feel attractive, alluring, feminine, and powerful somehow. I've never felt powerful at all, and I have the same unpowerful body, but right now I feel strong and confident somehow."

"*See?* That's what I've been trying to get you to feel. To feel the girl inside and how good she is for you. It's who you've always been, and now you've finally met her. I'll bet you're even ready for a man to make love to you." She gazed lovingly into my eyes, her thumb running circles on the back of my hand and her other hand on my thigh, slipping up and down my silky leg. Was I ready? I imagined it. I throbbed and throbbed over and over uncontrollably. Then I remembered what I was.

"Uh, god. It seems exciting but... but... I just can't fathom the thought of a man shoving himself in my butt and using me for his receptacle like that. It's as if I were in jail, and men would be using me for their depository."

"Oh, honey. Where do you get these images from? You're not a man in a jail. You're a powerful, sexy, confident, and alluring woman. You told me that's how you felt. You're a very pretty girl who decides who, when, and where a man gets to enjoy your assets. A girl who controls the men's pleasure as well as your own."

"Putting it that way sounds much better. But... I'm not quite ready."

"Okay. Well, let's go to the club, and we can see who's there for you to take care of. This time with those pretty lips. Okay?" Her hand slid on my hardness beneath my panties. "Mmm, I see you're feeling it well."

I nodded nervously and throbbed beneath her hand.

"Are you ready to enjoy the rewards you can bring with that pretty face and mouth?"

I throbbed in my panties over and over and over and felt myself ooze. I took her hand from my crotch. "God, yes. Please let me do that."

Alex looked around and waved the waiter over. She whispered to me, "Want to give him a nice tip?"

He dropped off the check and smiled at me. I smiled back. I shook my head. Alex said, "Thank you. It was a wonderful evening. Thanks so much." She picked up the check. He left. Alex turned to me. "He would have been a good one. He was hard for you. I saw it."

"I did too. He would have been for sure, but I think I need another drink at the club first. My heart is pounding."

"Okay. Relax first. No rush. Just tell me who and what you are now and what you intend to do tonight, okay, sweetie?" She signed the check, closed it, and put her credit card away. She held my hand and waited for my answer.

"My name is Billy. I'm Alex's wife, and I'm a sexy, powerful, and confident girl who's going to use her assets of lips and mouth on a real man, hopefully Peter, to reap a luscious reward of a man's passionate, lustful release because of my feminine allure. There. How was that?"

She kissed my lips. "Perfect."

9

While we waited outside for the valet, Alex texted on her phone. I had to ask, "Who's that, honey?"

"Just setting up proper plans in order to get my patient the best result, sweetheart."

"You work too hard."

She put her phone into her purse and smiled at me as she took my arm and pulled me close to her. "It's not hard. It's very rewarding when a patient finally becomes a full person. It's worth a little extra effort. Like you and your software patents. Same thing. We're both creators, right?"

"I never thought about it like that. I guess you're right."

The valet brought the car around, and Alex drove us off. I crossed and uncrossed my legs, adjusted my breasts, felt the silky sheer material of the bra on my hard nipples. My skin tingled all over. Rigid in my panties. I unconsciously caressed my silky stockinged legs as I looked out the passenger window and bounced a foot.

Alex reached across the console and slid her hand on my thigh, her long painted nails just touching my leg. "Need another libido pill for courage, honey?"

"Oh god, no. I'm ready."

"Good girl. It won't be long."

We got to the club, and I threw down the first martini and had a second gone soon after its arrival. I lifted the third one as we sat at the bar. The bartender laughed and said, "You better slow down, girl. Those are potent."

I nodded and smiled. "I know. I'll just sip this one now."

Alex's leg slid against mine under the bar, and she sipped her drink while picking at my hair with a finger. "I love all the colors and texture they put into your hair. It's so pretty. It really frames your face so well."

"Thanks. I like it too. It even feels nice to run my hand through it... or shake it." I shook my head and fluffed the layers.

Looking in the mirror behind the bar, I could see guys checking me out as they went past. I was afraid of meeting some weird stranger, though. Then it would feel like a jail scene or something.

Alex tapped my shoulder, and a grin filled her face; her eyes were bright and wide as she looked excitedly at me. "Oh surprise, surprise. How lucky can you get, girl? Look who's here, Billy. It's Dan, Mike, and Pete." She lifted herself in her chair and waved to them. They came over.

Pete immediately put his hand on my shoulder and looked me up and down. "You look stunning. Very sexy, Billy. This is you. If Alex hadn't said you were here with her, I may have not even recognized you. You're beautiful. May I kiss you?"

My face was flushed, I leaned toward him and offered a pucker. He placed a big hand on my thigh to lean in, then he kissed me lightly. He slid his hand. "Very sexy."

Dan and Mike were both waiting to say hello to me. They took turns and told me I should never go back to the old me. How stunning and gorgeous I was this way! How well it suited me. I was flattered with all the attention as Alex just sat there beaming and proud of me.

I started to feel the effects of the drinks, and my heart rate was slowing a bit. I turned my seat to face away from the bar and crossed my legs, bouncing a high-heeled foot, my stocking top just showing a bit. I enjoyed the attention from the men, their eyes flitting from cleavage to nipples in my now open crop top and shapely legs clad in sheer black stockings. I totally had them. They all had obvious hard-ons in their pants for me. I had never felt so attractive in my life. I was feeling good and having fun, something I hadn't done in a while.

With my new powerful, alluring, sexy, and confident persona, feeling like a million bucks and having these guys lusting for me, I knew it was time to take control. I pulled Pete down close and whispered. "I want to suck the juice out of you. Ready?"

Pete's eyes went wide, and he nodded. "If you want a little privacy, I own the club and we can use my office."

I slid off the barstool and slung my purse on my shoulder. Alex looked at me, one eyebrow raised.

"Uh, Pete and I are going to chat in his office. Do you have plans for Dan and Mike so we can meet after?"

"I do. I think we should all go to his office. If that's okay, Pete."

Pete nodded. "Excellent idea, Alex."

Pete led the way, holding my hand, and Alex followed with Dan and Mike. We entered the plush office, and Mike closed and locked the door behind us. Pete stood by the bar. "Drinks, anyone?" He mixed drinks for all the men and Alex. I passed since I was already far enough along. The guys stood against the bar, and Alex seated herself on the couch with her drink, which she placed on the end table. She took her phone from her purse. "I want a picture. Put Billy between all of you."

Pete wrapped his arm around my shoulder and Dan stood on the other side with Mike holding my hand. I put one foot in front of the other and showed some of the lace-top thigh-high, pointing my toe and lifting my heel. Alex took the shot.

Pete's hand rubbed my back. "Are there too many of us? Do you want more privacy?"

I looked around at the guys all ogling me. I looked at Alex. She raised her glass to me. "Get the show on the road, girl. You have three desperate men waiting for you."

My eyes popped wide as I realized she had set this up for me to service all of them. She tossed a pillow from the couch. "Kneel on that, honey. It'll be easier on your knees."

I took my lipstick from my purse and freshened it while looking into the reflection in my phone. Then I took the perfume from my purse, sprayed it all over me and put it back, putting the purse on the bar. I picked up the pillow and placed it before Pete.

He smiled down at me, unzipped his pants, and took out his shaved, silky, and very hard rod. He stroked it, looking at me. I was throbbing uncontrollably in my panties. I looked at the other guys and motioned to them. "C'mon now. Pay homage to me and do what Pete's doing—play with yourselves like little boys looking at porn, or you'll get nothing from me."

They all complied quickly, and I enjoyed watching them for a while as they just did that. They looked at me with lust in their eyes while they stroked their huge rods. I squeezed my breasts and licked my lips for them. They touched my hair, touched my lips, tried to gently move my mouth toward them.

I couldn't hold back any longer. I had to take command of these horny things. I went back and forth between the three of them, taking them in my mouth and tugging their shaved balls, stroking them sometimes with both hands and sometimes with one in each hand, going from one to the other. I was like a kid in a candy store. They were different in shape and size, but all of them were hard for me and loving my attention immensely.

I loved looking up into their eyes as they gazed lovingly down at me and put their hands in my hair, sometimes stroking it and sometimes tugging it with both hands, then thrusting into my face. I delighted in bringing them to the edge and making them wait while they oozed a drip from their tips and moaned little regrets that I didn't let them finish. I tortured them for what seemed forever. I loved every second of it. I was amazed one of them didn't get pissed at me and just stuff it in my pretty face.

I smelled their colognes from one to the other. Tasted their precums, felt their silky shafts on my lips and tongue. I left a lipstick ring on each of them at the farthest I could take them into my mouth. I tugged on their balls and rolled them in my fingers, ran my nails under them, driving them wild. I was oozing and throbbing in my panties and on the edge myself. My skin tingled; my nipples rubbed the fabric of my bra. I couldn't last much longer. Besides, I desperately wanted to make them come for me.

I decided to save Pete for last. Dan was first. I looked up at him as I stroked him. "Ready to give me my reward, Dan?" He gave a crooked grin and placed both hands on my head, squeezing it while he looked into my eyes. "Oh yeah, little sissy girl."

I took him into my mouth and went at it with fervor. Lips, tongue, stroking, tugging, running my tongue around his shaft and flicking the tip. He shuddered and shook and held my head tighter, then began to make little thrusts into my face while looking into my eyes.

I felt him swell in my mouth, and the first gush filled it. Looking into his eyes, I swallowed, and the next gush came. He slid out a little and back in, and I swallowed some more. He slid out again and popped loose, sending a pearly stream in the air above me. I dove back on it and made him give me every drop, his knees shaking, until he had to pull my head off him.

I went to Mike, nodded at him and stroked him as I looked up at him. "Put your hands behind your back and keep them there, Mike." He did. I told Pete, "Watch me and bring yourself to the edge, then I'll do you last."

I went crazy on Mike. He tried to hump into my face, but I moved my head with it and tortured him until I was ready to make him let it go. Then I grabbed the base of his thick cock tight and went wild on it. I had him gushing in a flash, and I swallowed voraciously but had to pop off for a second or choke. His big dick ripped a surge of cream across my dress and breasts before I retrieved the spasming beast back into my mouth. Again, like Dan, I drained him until there was no more, and he had to pull me off.

Pete was looking at me while playing with his long, thick, and veiny dick. It was oozing from the nearly purple head, and he was stroking it fast. Then he stopped and let it bounce in the air and drip. I moved toward it and grasped it lightly, then wrapped my lips around the head and looked up at him. He spurted in my mouth immediately. His eyes rolled in his head, and he pushed it into my face.

I backed off it and swallowed, looking up at his eyes, but it slipped out and shot a rope across my cheek and forehead before I got it back into my mouth. He twisted my hair in his fingers and fucked my face, shooting the rest of his load into me while grunting and calling my name. I came in my panties and shook all over. His cum dribbled from my mouth, and I licked it up before collapsing on the ground. I was swept up from the floor in strong arms and placed on the couch.

10

I heard Alex talking. "Just take her out the back door and put her in my car for me. She's *done* for tonight. I need to get her home."

Someone lifted me from the couch and carried me out. I opened my eyes and wrapped my arm around Pete's shoulders, trying to see where we were going. I snuggled into his neck and breathed in his cologne. "God, Pete, that was incredible. It took everything out of me."

"You were incredible; so driven, passionate, and in control. See? A meant-to-be. You've been missing so much all this time not being you."

"Mmm." He lowered me to my feet next to the car, and I slid into the passenger seat and he closed the door. Alex got behind the wheel, and we drove off. "Good girl, Billy. Seems you've shown your true colors, girl. Only one more infusion, and you'll be certain there's no turning back. You're a girl."

"I'm still not quite ready for that, Alex. I have to admit, it was really something doing that for those guys. Something incredible. Wild. I've never felt so driven. I never thought I'd be doing something I used to think was disgusting. Never. Yet right now, I feel proud, accomplished, powerful."

"Excellent. Those are all the things you feel when you're doing and being who you are inside. Give some thought to the next step. Remember how good I felt when it happened to me. How you could almost feel my pleasure yourself. That's a big part of why you love to watch. You see how wonderful it is and subconsciously you want to immerse yourself in that feeling. You'll get there, honey. It's totally natural for you to. It's going to be fine." She rubbed my hand and shot a quick glance at me as we passed under a streetlight.

"Billy, wait until you see how you look. I didn't notice when I was videoing you, but the boys left a lot of badges on you to prove your accomplishments."

I pulled down the visor and it lit up. My hair, face, cheeks—all were covered with the results of my ministrations. I looked down at my chest. Cleavage, dress, all with more evidence. I was somehow shocked now at what I had done. I hurriedly took tissues from the console and began frantically wiping it all up.

11

I slept fitfully and must have humped my pillow a few times because I woke with it between my legs, and it was damp. Alex planted a kiss on my forehead as she leaned on her elbow, gazing at me. She ran her hand through my hair. "Hello, princess. Time for breakfast and your vitamins." She kissed me lightly on the lips. "Rise and shine, sexy girl."

I slid out of bed, my babydoll nightie and its panties damp. I slid into my fuzzy, heeled mule slippers and went into the bathroom. I brushed my teeth and threw my clothes into the hamper, then put on pink panties and tied a short pink satin robe around me. I went into the kitchen.

Alex was making breakfast and had all my vitamins laid out. I sat in my chair. "I don't want the libido pill, Alex. I can't stop. It's too much. It's not real. I want to feel what I feel and not be influenced by that pill anymore. Please?" I moved the pill to the side.

"If you like, sweetie. I thought it was helping you, and I think you should still take it for now, but if you don't want it, that's fine too. You'll still have a normal libido, which will work fine." She put the French toast in front of us and kissed my forehead, then sat down.

"Thanks." I took my other vitamins with my grapefruit juice and started eating.

Alex said, "Okay. Now for you to finish your immersion into being a woman, you know what you need to do next."

I rolled my eyes and savored the sweet, gushy toast. I nodded.

"Good. It isn't something to be feared or avoided, and I want you to be open and excited about it. I want you to be looking forward to it, not afraid if it. How can I help you to get there?"

I looked up at the ceiling, giving it some thought. The jail scene kept popping into my mind. I whined a little, "Somehow I still feel like a femboy in jail and that real men are just gonna use me as a receptacle. That's disturbing the mood. It's hard to get motivated with that image looming."

"Okay. Hmm, how do we make it so you don't feel like an femboy being abused? Well, one is you're a girl, not a boy. That has to come into play so we can eliminate that feeling, right?"

I nodded. "I guess. I mean I shouldn't feel like a femboy anymore as it is. I look like a genetic woman now. Maybe those feelings will change with time?"

"They will. Hmm. When we were married, you were a mini version of a male groom. You've always been a male with feminine traits, and that was your self-image. You tried to minimize the feminine and emphasize the male aspects, but you retained a certain femininity all the time."

I nodded and chewed, looking at her beautiful, bright eyes.

"How about we reestablish our wedding vows with both of us as brides this time? We could have a small wedding and reception, and then we could consummate our vows together."

"Consummate our vows like we did on our wedding night? That was a very short consummation, if I remember correctly. You were way too exciting for me. I'd love to try that again."

"Well, I was thinking of something more modern, more open. You know, like the way you help me fulfill my desires. This time, though, we'd have some help filling both of our desires, side by side, holding hands, gazing into each other's eyes. Two brides in love, enjoying each other's pleasure being given to us by helpful, motivated, lusting men. Two brides being bred side by side on their wedding night. I'd be right alongside you..." She reached out and held my hand, "...holding your hand while we both receive our wedding night inseminations."

I imagined the scene. Alex right next to me while a real man takes her to heaven as she holds my hand. That sounded wonderful. Then I imagined the same thing being done to me at the same time. I pictured Pete and me, intimately connected while he drives himself into me over and over, my wife holding my hand while Dan or someone else fills her up and stuffs her to bliss, dumping his passion deep inside of her. I throbbed in my robe, my face flushed. A little grin slid onto my face, even though I tried to hide it.

Alex wore an ear-to-ear smile. "Oh my! I think you've turned into a blushing bride, Billy." She reached across and squeezed my hand. "I love you, honey. I'll take care of everything."

"Uh...I uh..."

12

We cleaned up our breakfast dishes, had coffee on the patio, and then I showered.

"Alex, want to see the video of you and the boys?"

"Uh, can you delete that please?"

"I will. I just thought you might like to see how sexy you were. You know, to help reinforce your self-image a bit as an attractive, alluring, highly desired woman." She sat by me as I dried my hair with a towel on the bed, getting ready to go shopping with her.

I couldn't *not* look at it as she turned the phone sideways and the sound played. The guys were really into me, and I was really into them. Alex slid my panties aside and placed my thumb and forefinger on my shaft. "Go ahead, honey. Jerk your sissy cock. Watch and remember how good it was. Remember how much you love sucking real men's cocks. Jerk that little sissy thing of yours with your thumb and forefinger and show me how much of a sissy you are by making it squirt while watching yourself sucking off real men. It's who you are, princess."

She handed me the phone so I could hold it. I could have stopped it, but I didn't. I sat there jerking myself while Alex got dressed and watched me. I watched myself sucking and playing with them all and could see how they were all reacting. It was incredibly exciting seeing myself as if it were someone else. But it wasn't. It was me, all me. I remembered my excitement, and I jerked myself frantically with two fingers and my thumb. My breath was coming in gasps; little whimpers issued from me. My body tingled.

"Good girl, Billy, that's it. Watch yourself be the hot girl pleasing the real men. Pump that little twink of yours and make it spurt." She sat next to me and held her palm in front of my shaft. Go ahead, honey. When Pete shoots, I want you to shoot as well, just like you did then."

Her hand ran circles on my back through the satin robe, and her other hand squeezed my breast and pinched my nipple. I watched the video of Pete as he reached the edge, then began erupting. I whimpered. Alex put her palm in front of it, and I squirted into her hand over and over, my body shaking. "Good girl, Billy. Good girl. That's it, get it all out so it can rest and go soft, and you can relax and get dressed. Go on. I think there's a little more." I jerked it furiously, my face contorted, and another squirt came out. "That's it, baby. Such a good girl."

She lifted the palm of her hand and fed it to me. I lapped it up greedily, remembering getting my rewards before and how proud I was. I fell back on the bed to catch my breath. In a few moments, I felt Alex putting the cage being back on me.

"Alex!"

"Shush now." She lifted me up, slid two pills into my mouth, and handed me a glass of water. Take your medicine."

I swallowed them down.

"Good girl. A double dose just to get you saturated, and then one every four hours, except when you're sleeping, until you fulfill your mission."

"Alex! Please!" I lowered my head and gave her doe eyes, ready to cry.

"Oh, Billy, be a big girl. You know you'll be faster to accept our wedding night this way. You'll be so looking forward to it after a few days."

"A few days?"

"Of course. We won't be able to pull it together until the weekend. Besides, we need to put together our bridal outfits." She took her phone out and started the cage's e-stim program.

"I shuddered. Too much!"

She looked at me and adjusted it. "There."

"Gosh, Alex. A few days with this and the pills too? At least I'm not plugged."

"Uh, not yet, but you will be every day during the day. Now go and put in your plug like a proper sissy and pump it up really well so you can get used to something as large as Peter in you. You want to be ready for him, don't you? You want him to fit, right?"

I nodded quickly.

"Of course you do." She winked, stood, and held her hand out to help me off the bed. "Go plug and get dressed to go shopping. Wear some really high heels like you'll be wearing for the wedding so you can see how the dresses will look."

I stood there, the e-stim making me swell in the cage, the pills already making it more demanding. I rubbed my breasts and squeezed my nipples. "High heels sound nice right now for some reason." I went and plugged.

13

I did my hair and makeup and decided to go for a classy look in one of Alex's gray pinstripe skirt-suits with a pair of super high-heeled, open-toe, patent leather shoes, sheer suntan pantyhose with a piece of the crotch cut out, and a pair of stretchy black lace panties holding my cage lock from clicking with every step. A black shelf bra allowed a cream-colored satin V-neck blouse to caress my hard nipples with each step, as my breasts jiggled from my mincing steps in the heels. Bejeweled and perfumed, I felt like a million bucks.

Alex came into the bedroom as I was inspecting myself in the mirror. "You look stunning. Very professional and classy." She gave me a kiss on the cheek. "Feeling good?"

"If being on the edge and horny as hell is feeling good, then I'm one hundred percent. Please, can I at least take the plug out?"

"Not yet. Later. I want to show you something." She led me into the spare room and went into the closet. She held her wedding gown out in front of me. "Want to wear my wedding gown for your insemination night? Then you can feel like a real bride. The skirt opens in front if you remember."

I held it and let the fluffy crinoline brush my hand. The beading on the V-neck top was gorgeous, as was the full, trailing hem of the dress. It was like a dream. "It's so lovely. I remember seeing you in it with your long veil as you came down the aisle."

She smiled. "It's yours. I'll just get something simple for myself. You're the virgin."

"Don't you want to wear it?"

"I'd rather see you in it. We don't have time to have another made, but I can find something off the shelf. Let's go get all the other accoutrements and underthings for you and find a dress for me. Okay?"

"Okay." I took Alex's hand, and she led me through the house to the garage. Each step moved the plug in me and jiggled my breasts, rubbing my nipples on the silky top. There wasn't a motion I made that didn't add to my arousal.

On the way out, Alex gave me another pill to take.

"I don't need this."

"I don't care."

We spent the day shopping and found a sexy bride's dress for Alex that fit her perfectly. It was very short and had a revealing top. She bought a veil and garters, sheer white lace-top stockings for us both, along with strappy, beaded white stilettos with five-and-a-half-inch heels. Walking in them meant taking miniscule steps. It felt vulnerable and feminine as hell.

By the end of the day, we had all we needed, and Alex had found a JP to do the ceremony. The wedding would be in our garden in the backyard, and a rented tent would provide shelter for the seating and tables. The planning was done. We were ready.

We stopped at a nice bar on the way home for a drink. I slid onto the barstool and wriggled onto my plug while the cage's e-stim shot off. I crossed my silky legs. Our martinis arrived, and Alex held hers up to me. "To Billy's wedding night."

I clinked glasses with her. "To our wedding night." We sipped. "Alex, can I please stop with the plug and cage and pills? I can't survive much longer like this, and I will definitely not last two more days this way. I'm ready now. I feel it. I want Pete to make love to me while you hold my hand. The plug is bigger than Pete or any man on this earth right now. Pete will fit in me easily. Please stop this torture!"

"Hmm." She sipped. She looked around the empty bar. "You sure? I mean absolutely sure? No fears, no hesitancy?"

"I can't wait to wear your wedding dress and renew our vows. I can't wait to see you made love to while I have the same done to me as we hold hands. Honest. I mean it. I want it." I ran my long-nailed hand on her silky stockinged thigh and gazed into her eyes. "I love you and want to turn the page on our new lives. I want to be a woman and have a man make love to me just like I've seen real men do to you. I want to be a perfect wife and be inseminated by real men the way you always are."

"Okay." She dug in her purse. "Here." She handed me the key to the cage. "And you can just pitch the plug. It's served its purpose. Put the cage in your purse."

My eyes popped wide open, and a smile came over my face from ear to ear. I stood and peppered her face with kisses, then ran off to the girls' room. It felt so good to be free of the cage and e-stim and to not have the plug sending cycles of vibrations into me. I dried my twinkie off and tucked it into my panties. I was no less horny, but I was much more comfortable and less edgy.

I walked back to the bar, took my seat, crossed my legs, and took a deep breath. "Thank you. I feel so much better. Now let me stop taking the pills, okay?"

"Okay, sweetie. I trust you." She kissed my lips. The bartender came over, and we ordered another round before dinner. We chatted about the wedding and what it was going to be like for me to be taken by Pete. She didn't miss a single graphic, sensual detail of how it would feel—or how I would feel. She left me beside myself with desire for a real man to take me that way. I was oozing in my panties.

Alex snuggled in close and brushed her silky leg against mine. She slid her hand under my skirt and stroked me through my panties. It wasn't a second before I erupted and soaked them and the slip under my skirt.

I looked around quickly. No one had seen us. I placed my hand on Alex's silky thigh and squeezed it. "God! Thank you, Alex. Finally, I can relax a little. You got me so worked up talking about what it would be like for me."

I recrossed my legs, trapping the dampness between my thighs. I looked around the bar again, my heart slowing to a normal pace now.

Alex squeezed my hand on the bar. "I love you, Billy! You are the sweetest little girl I've ever known. Yes, you deserve to relax a little before your big day." She took a pill from her purse and crushed it between her thumb and forefinger into my martini.

"Alex!? I don't want another libido pill."

"Sorry, sweetie. I love seeing you like this. Drink your martini and relax while you can."

14

That was the last pill, and Alex let me bring myself to release three more times that night while she narrated scenes from our wedding night to come and I rode on a dildo facing her. I slept very well.

Our waiting days were heavenly. To be the new me and be unencumbered by a ridiculous libido yet feel feminine, pretty, and confident—all the new feelings that came with the new me—was heavenly. I was truly excited for both of us to renew our vows and to consummate our marriage in such an open and sharing way. The morning of our wedding day came quickly.

I woke in bed with a raging hard-on and took my shower, but I didn't let myself release. Alex told me to be good and save it for later when it would be more enticing.

I dressed in the white stockings and garter belt, white lace and beaded panties, white shelf bra, garters, and heels. I sat on the bed to affix my fetishy high wedding heels on my ankles. When I finished, Alex was already dressed in her short wedding dress and came over to me. "Stand up."

I did. She pulled down and removed my panties and proceeded to decorate my leaping twinkie. She slid up crotchless, ruffled and beaded lace panties, then wrapped a white lace garter around my globes and shaft. She twisted it and wrapped it around my globes again, making the whole package stand out. Next, she decorated the crotchless panties with pink and white flowers all around the upper edge and then wrapped a silky soft ribbon under the globes and around the base of my shaft and tied a pretty bow.

She stood back and admired her work. "There! Doesn't it look so insignificant, cute, and feminine now? And it'll be held up and out against the soft crinoline in your dress. You'll love the feeling of the fluffiness against it. Put on your dress and see."

I looked down at it all as my twinkie voluntarily lifted and fell over and over. "It is cute. Very cute. So insignificant now. It looks so girlie and pretty. Very sissy."

"See? I knew you'd like that, being the girly sissy girl you are now. Put on your dress."

I finished dressing; Alex helped me with my veil, and I helped her. It was wonderful sharing the experience of being a bride with my wife. I practiced walking with the dress, holding the hem up to climb stairs, collecting the train to make a turn. The crinoline made it feel as if my twink were nested in a cloud. It was oozing and leaping steadily in its cloudlike haven.

"I feel like an angel, honey. Thanks for letting me wear your dress." She fussed with my veil and sprayed perfume all over me and under my dress. She adjusted my earrings and jewelry and tied white lace ribbons around my ankles above the stilettos, making them look even more fetishy. "Are you about done, Alex? I mean, I can't get more feminine, can I?"

"Well, do you feel feminine and ready for a real man to take you as a bride?"

"Oh god, yes."

"Good, let's go outside and have a drink before they all arrive."

We made our way down the stairs and out without me taking a tumble. We made martinis and sat in the shade. Alex offered me a cigarette. "Emergency smoke?"

"Yes, please."

She lit it for me, and I took a deep drag and blew it out. Pink lipstick stained the end of the filter. "God, why am I so nervous?"

"It's your wedding day, girl. You've never been a wife before. You *should* be excited."

I adjusted my dress so I could cross my legs, and I bounced one leg over the other in my silky white stockings while my decorated twinkie leapt and fell. I sipped my drink and took another puff. I thought about the men.

"This is almost too exciting for me. I hope I don't faint."

"You won't. Just take deep breaths and relax. Sip your drink." She rubbed my lace-gloved arm and gazed into my eyes. "So pretty. So feminine."

"Thanks."

The first of the guests arrived. I didn't recognize them. They came over to us, flashing white teeth behind dark brown skin. They introduced themselves with deep voices. The one had his eyes locked on me while he smiled and said, "Dan said this was the place. He said there were brides in need of service. I imagine you're the two young ladies."

Alex spoke up and he turned to her. "Uh, yes." She looked at me. "Billy, I asked Dan to bring what he thought I'd most like as a gift but not to buy anything for us or give us money or things." She looked back and forth at the two of them. "I guess this is Dan's gift to me?"

"Yes, ma'am. We are your gift… if that's okay. He said we should plan on spending plenty of time to take care of you on your wedding night. Is this good?"

Alex laughed. "What should I say, Billy?"

"Say what I know you should. Dan made a good choice."

She turned back to them. "This is literally fucking fantastic, guys. I can't wait." She motioned to them. "Help yourself to drinks and snacks, gentlemen."

We looked to the side entrance, and there were two young, thin, slimly built men, maybe in their early twenties, holding hands, smiling, and walking toward us across the grass. Alex leaned over to me. "Oh my! Aren't they a couple of cute little femboys!"

Behind them were two hot young women. "Billy, that's Trisha and Chelsea. They're two trannies I did some counseling for before. Some of Dan's old friends."

Behind them followed Mike, Dan, and Pete, along with the justice of the peace carrying his book.

I finished my drink and looked into Alex's eyes. She laughed a bit. "Don't be so nervous, honey. I'll get you another drink. Just sit here and look pretty."

15

We all ate and had drinks until it was time for the JP to do the ceremony. "Here Comes the Bride" played, and Alex walked down the aisle on Dan's arm, followed by me on Pete's arm, our veils draped over our faces. When we reached the podium, we were presented to each other and stood side by side before the JP.

He introduced himself and lifted our veils. "Welcome to all of you and thank you for joining us to celebrate renewing the vows of Alex and Billy. Alex, hold Billy's hands and look into her eyes, and you may state your vows to her.

"Billy, I love you and will cherish you forever. I will develop you and support you as my wife, whom I will honor, cherish, guide, and strive to make into the most fulfilled, lovely, stunning woman a wife could ever have for a wife. I look forward to sharing our lives together, pursuing all there is to enjoy in this world." Alex turned to the JP.

The JP nodded. "Billy?"

I held her hands and gazed into her eyes. "Alex, I love you and will cherish you forever. I will obediently take your guidance to become the perfect wife for you and to become the person I am meant to be. I will honor, cherish, obey, and strive to give you all the wonderful things, both physical and mental, in order that you may be proud of me and forever thankful to have me as your wife."

"Do you, Billy, take Alex to be your lawfully wedded wife?"

"I do."

"Do you, Alex, take Billy to be your lawfully wedded wife?"

"I do."

"Then the brides may kiss."

Alex wrapped her arms around me and dipped me back as she gave me a deep kiss on my lips. The crowd hooted and hollered and clapped. Alex turned us toward the JP and in a swift move, she yanked the front panel off my gown. I cried out, "Alex!?" She turned us to the crowd, and we bowed. My face turned beet-red. I looked at my twinkie as it leapt up and down in its nest of flowers and ruffles. The crowd applauded.

I leaned into Alex and whispered, "Why did you do that?"

"You look so sweet that way with your little twinkie dancing in its tiny nest. Remember when I wore the dress and took that off for the reception, and how much our guests loved it? It'll be so much easier to move in, anyway. Just relax and follow the vows you just took. Be a big girl."

I looked around, my heart racing. Dan and Pete brought us drinks. "You girls look stunning. Especially you, Billy. You'd never be mistaken for a man. Your little nest shows how feminine you really are," Dan said as he put an arm around my wife. "And Alex here—she always makes me hard for her." He kissed her deeply on the lips and squeezed her breast as he did.

Pete put his arm around me and crushed me to him. "So young lady, how does it feel to be a blushing bride? Are you ready for your wedding celebration?"

I shook my head and looked down. My twinkie had retreated into the nest from my shock. "Not quite yet. That was a bit of a surprise for me, and I'm still getting over it."

"Don't worry. Have some of your drink and you'll be as good as new." He kissed me on the lips, cradling my head and squeezing my breast. I leaned back and looked into his eyes. He placed my gloved hand on his crotch. "Feel how hard you make me?"

I rubbed it and immediately began to rise from the nest. "Mmm, that does feel nice."

Alex came over and took my hand, placing three pills in my palm. "I think you should take these. If you finish accidentally, it won't matter because you'll stay ready for another."

"That's okay. I'll behave until it's time for Pete and me and you and Dan."

"Oh, Billy, but there is so much more. Take them for me now, honey." She handed me her martini. I popped them and slugged it down. "Good girl."

We all ate and drank, and Alex and I mingled a while. We sat at a table with the two trans girls. They were both gorgeous and sexy, and you'd never know they had a secret beneath their minidresses.

Alex said, "Trisha and Chelsea have been together from the time they were just femboys in high school. Don't they make a stunning couple, Billy?"

I nodded and sipped my drink, my twinkie leaping and falling under the fluff of my dress I had pulled over my knee. "Yes, you two make a stunning couple."

"Billy, why don't you be a good girl and show the girls how good you are with your mouth and lips. Why don't you get on your knees and take care of them?" Alex turned to them. "Ladies? Would that be pleasant?"

They looked at each other and grinned, then looked at me, smiling. "Only if Billy wants to."

Alex motioned with her head, and I got onto my knees in front of Trisha. She slid the tight hem of her minidress up, showing a packed pair of black lace panties.

Alex stood. "I'll go get the girls some cake and another drink while you show them your hospitality, honey." She left the table, and Trisha gently pulled my head toward her. I moved closer on my knees and took her into my mouth. She was huge, to say the least. Her perfume smelled incredible. I wrapped one hand around the base and began bobbing my head, running my tongue around it. I occasionally flicked the tip with my tongue, loving the response I got.

Chelsea moved her chair closer and lifted the hem of her dress, pulling the panties aside and making herself available to me. I went to her next and began my mission, enjoying every moment. She was much smaller than Trisha, and the contrast between the two was delightful.

Alex brought them cake and drinks on a tray, and they began eating and drinking while they watched me go back and forth between them. The two gorgeous black men came over and stood watching as I ministered to Trisha and Chelsea. They both took out their huge, intimidating shafts and stroked them with their big hands as they watched me. One said, "Very nice, Billy. It seems you've found your calling in life."

Alex stood alongside him. She grabbed his shaft in her hand and stroked it for him. "She sure has. Isn't it amazing how much she loves doing this? I mean, to me, it's nice to do, but to her, it's the elixir of life. And look how dedicated and passionate she is. She's the perfect little sissy, isn't she?"

I glared at Alex as I gobbled up Trisha.

Alex laughed. "Oh, don't be so sensitive. You *know* you are. Just enjoy it and be yourself."

And I did enjoy it. Every second. I was about to make Trisha finish and give me her reward when one of the big black men lifted me up and put me on the table. "Here ya go, Trish. It's time for her first breeding. Right, Alex?"

"Oh yes. Long overdue."

He hurriedly pulled my skirt aside, lifted my legs back, and slid my crotchless panties to the side. His friend held one leg, and he held the other as Trisha slid me to the edge of the table and pressed her thick shaft into my bottom making me gasp and squeak. She furiously humped into me, shaking the table. The two big men held me fast, and one turned my head and shoved his thick shaft into my face.

He held my head tight and thrusted into it while Trisha let out a little moan. I felt her swell and shrink while her thick rod spasmed inside me and pumped her reward deep. Trisha pulled out, and Chelsea replaced her in an instant, making me gasp again as she filled me.

She pounded me hard and fast, making me whimper and shake around the cock in my mouth. Then Chelsea turned my head off the cock and looked into my eyes while her rod swelled and shrunk in me, depositing her passion. The one from my mouth quickly got between my legs. He slowly worked his ridiculously large rod into me as my eyes opened wide. I held my breath as it slowly impaled me.

Alex brushed my locks off my forehead and kissed it. "That's it, Billy. Just relax now, and soon, he'll be all the way in. Good girl."

I looked at his eyes as he watched my expression carefully. Once he had breached my gate, I let out a deep breath, and he pushed it all the way in. He began to stroke into me slowly. I looked to Alex. She smiled and kissed my forehead. "You're doing really well, honey. How does it feel to be a woman with a real man inside you?"

I rolled my eyes. My little twinkie was leaping and oozing with each thrust he made. Alex sat on the table next to me and pulled the other big black guy over to her. She held his long shaft as she guided him into her.

He began to pound her, making the table shake. Alex took my hand and held it tight as she looked into my eyes. "Oh, Billy. This feels so good, doesn't it, honey? Don't you love seeing your wife with a real man to make her happy while another real man uses you as his sissy girl?"

I nodded and rolled my eyes, my head shaking from each thrust of the big black rod inside me.

Alex looked to him. "Now dump it into that little sissy's butt. Stuff her with it. Use her up." He nodded and grunted, then stuffed it all the way in.

I gasped and whimpered, "God, that's good." Alex held my hand tight as the man grunted and reamed me as she had asked, pounding me into the table and stuffing it up to my throat. He held it there as it pumped and gushed into me. Alex shook and shuddered as she pulled the bottom of the guy inside her to her and came on his huge cock gushing deep in her.

When they were both finished, Pete and Dan swept us up and took us into our bedroom. Mike followed behind. Dan promptly placed Alex on the satin sheets, stripped all his clothes off, and spread her legs, shoving it hard and deep into her. She wrapped her high-heeled legs around his waist and hung onto him.

Pete and Mike stripped down to their perfectly shaved, muscled frames, both with standing rods before them. Pete spread my legs and pushed them back, then quickly slid it deliciously into the depth of my wanton soul. I whimpered, "Oh yes, Pete. You feel the best of all of them. I feel so connected to you honey." Mike grabbed my head and put my mouth onto him, using my head like a Fleshlight. Pete became a beast and put all his masculine energy into me.

I lay there being pummeled, an electric current running from head to toe, sending blissful, erotic energy coursing through my body with each thrust into my face and butt. I felt Alex grab my hand and squeeze it, and I turned my head slightly to see her looking at me as Dan gave her another fierce shudder and shake. He was shaking the bed, and Pete tried to get in time with him as he skewered me on his shaft. They got in sync, even Mike in my face.

I rode a wave of sensation, and it seemed I was adrift in a sea of pleasure. I could see myself lying on the bed alongside Alex as we both were given our bridal breeding. I watched as if it were a movie. I felt every thrust and ripple; my twinkie oozed and flailed in little circles, flinging drops into the air before me.

Alex squeezed my hand tight and commanded, "Now, Pete and Mike. Now is the time. Fill that sissy up with your passionate releases. Pete, breed your bride. Dan, breed me in front of my spouse. Dump your real man's luscious load it into me."

They all began grunting and pounding. I glanced at my wife in all her glory and bliss. Mike moved my head and thrusted his shaft, making me guard my teeth and squeeze him with my lips. I ran my tongue around his shaft while he used me, and Pete shoved hard and deep. I was at the precipice of a mountain when I saw all five of us on the bed. Alex and I were like offerings to the gods as the god-like beasts took their pleasure from us and gave us heaven.

Grunts and groans, and they all tensed and shoved. Alex squeezed my hand tight and let out a howl before her whole body shuddered and shook; Dan's thick glistening shaft spasmed and pumped itself into her. I could see it pulsing as it spewed and she shook, squeezing my hand tight. Her telling eyes met mine.

Pete and Mike were both tensed up as they, too, swelled and pumped into me. My little bird in its nest spewed and flailed in the air, shooting strings out across my belly and breasts.

We all stopped moving. Alèx slid close to me and peppered my cheek with kisses. I then noticed several people in the bedroom with us. The cute femboys were standing facing each other, their cocks rubbing together in one of their hands as they humped into it and they looked at us. They came closer as well as a few other guys we hadn't seen yet. I smiled at the femboys; they were so cute. They seemed to ask permission as they came closer, and one held my hand. I nodded.

They both turned to us and grabbed their cocks, shaking at their knees as they spent streams out onto our faces and hair. The others in the room came over as well, and one wrapped my hair around it, and another did the same with Alex's hair and they came that way in our hair and faces. When they were all done, we were covered in their rewards, and I was jerking my little birdie while Alex was once again being pounded, but this time by Mike. I watched, and with two fingers and my thumb, I jerked quickly, sitting on the bed next to my wife and watching a real man service her properly until she came. I came when they did. Mike retreated and everybody left our room.

16

That night we just showered, put on our nightclothes and fell fast asleep in the crisp, clean sheets of the spare bedroom. I woke to Alex snuggled against me, the sweet skin of her cheek by my nose. I moved close and wrapped my leg over hers and slid my panties against her thigh. Her eyes opened, and she smiled. "Morning, my wife."

"Morning, my wife." I pressed myself against her leg and humped it slowly. "Mmm, it feels so good to be next to you like this. This is all I want; this is all I need."

"Really? That's all?"

"It could be."

She nodded. "It is the best part. So. How was your experience yesterday? Did it fulfill all your desires?"

"Mmm, God, yes. And some. And you?"

"It was very special. You know, we could both retire and just travel the world and have different experiences now. We have plenty of money. Would you like that? We could even find other people like you and help them become who they are. That might be rewarding."

"I suppose it would. I'd like to help other girls like me become who they are." I slid against her silky leg and kissed her forehead. "I'd like to get some implants, though, and have a shapelier body. I kinda like being a little sex kitten. I'd like to look more like you. Maybe even shapelier and sluttier, with bigger breasts and hips and butt and maybe enhanced lips and cheeks too... I'd like to become a totally slutty bimbo-like girl—if you'd let me."

"Sounds like fun! Okay. Consider it done. That, and *then* we travel and make more new girls, just like you."

"Deal." The thought of it really began to entice me. I reached down, slid my panties aside, and stroked myself against Alex's leg. "I, uh... Can I..."

"What? Go ahead. Jerk it off like a good little sissy girl. Go ahead."

"Well, I meant... can I..." I slid it across her thigh and lifted myself over her other leg, straddling her. "Can I... Could I please, maybe..."

"Ah, I see. You want to do it like a real man would, huh, honey?"

I nodded.

"Go ahead, princess. You try if you can. That's fine. It won't take long. It's so cute when you try to do that. See if you can try to keep it in me. I'd like to actually *feel you* in me when you finish." She slid her legs back, pulling her panties aside. I nervously moved forward, full of excitement, my rod leaping and oozing in anticipation. I pressed her legs back as far as they would go to make it easier to reach it.

She looked at it as it leapt and oozed. "I do remember the feeling when you managed to keep it in and you finished in me, and it's so cute and endearing when it happens. Simply adorable. Maybe just push it in quickly so it's *in* before you finish and don't even *try* to thrust so it doesn't have a chance to fall out. Okay, little girl?"

I nodded quickly while I was dying with anticipation. I could feel the inevitable coming quickly. I whimpered. "Hurry, please. Before it's too late."

She grasped it gingerly with her thumb and forefinger and guided me to her. I hurriedly struggled to get close enough, and she managed to get the tip into that tight, hot, wet space. She looked into my eyes and held her hand on my neck. "Go ahead, princess. Take me like all the real men did yesterday."

I managed to get it in all the way, feeling her tightness engulf the full length, and my body tensed. I whimpered as I shoved it in as hard as I could and held it there, our pelvises touching. It gushed and pumped. I thrusted, and the tip slid out, and it shot onto her belly. I struggled to get it back in before it was over and managed to have the tip in her for the last couple spasms.

I rolled onto my back, gasping for air. Alex rolled on top of me and looked down at me as she squeezed my breast and planted a kiss on my lips. "A valiant effort my love. You almost kept it the whole time. I love you, my little sissy girl, Billy. Next time no thrusting, just be happy you got it in there and hold it there like the real men do at the end. You've seen them do that to me so do it like them. Skip the thrusting like they do though, because you'll pop out and so that doesn't work for you? We know that, right?"

I nodded quickly and sheepishly. "Yes dear. I know dear. Ill try better next time. I gazed into her gorgeous eyes. "I love you so much, Alex."

"I know my adorable dear. I know." She cradled my head.

56

If you enjoyed this book, it would be great if you could leave a review and tell a friend about it, or blog it out. Thanks!
Barb and Thom
For more of books, both fiction and non-fiction, go to:
Amazon:
http://www.amazon.com/Barbara-Deloto/e/B00J21HWA4/